PEANUTS

By **Charles M. Schulz**   Illustrated by **Robert Pope**

Countdown to Christmas!

With a Story a Day

SIMON SPOTLIGHT
An imprint of Simon & Schuster Children's Publishing Division
New York   London   Toronto   Sydney   New Delhi
1230 Avenue of the Americas, New York, New York 10020
This Simon Spotlight edition September 2021
Peanuts and all related titles, logos, and characters are trademarks of Peanuts Worldwide LLC
© 2021 Peanuts Worldwide LLC.
See next page for individual copyright and writing credits.
All rights reserved, including the right of reproduction in whole or in part in any form.
SIMON SPOTLIGHT and colophon are registered trademarks of Simon & Schuster, Inc.
For information about special discounts for bulk purchases, please contact
Simon & Schuster Special Sales at 1-866-506-1949 or business@simonandschuster.com.
Manufactured in China 0122 SCP
2 4 6 8 10 9 7 5 3
ISBN 978-1-5344-9698-9
ISBN 978-1-5344-9699-6 (ebook)

This book belongs to:

_____

A Story for
December 1

Mix-Up at the North Pole

Bells jingled, lights twinkled, and the feeling of Christmas was in the air. Everyone was excited for the holiday season. That is, everyone except Charlie Brown. "This is going to be a dreadful Christmas," he sighed.

Marcie looked surprised. "Why do you say that?" she asked.

Charlie Brown pulled out a stack of envelopes from his coat pocket.

He sadly looked down at the letters. They were all addressed to Santa Claus.

"I told Santa Claus about how I've been very good this year," Charlie Brown explained. He made his bed every day, helped Sally with her homework, and always remembered to feed Snoopy on time!

"That sounds like you've been well behaved," Marcie said.

"Well, I guess Santa Claus didn't think so. All my letters came back unopened!" he wailed.

Marcie examined the letters. Sure enough, the envelopes were still completely sealed. Each one had a big, black stamp on the front: RETURN TO SENDER.

Marcie looked closer at the envelopes. Then her eyes widened. "Don't worry, Charles! You still have a chance to have a wonderful Christmas," she said. "You just sent these letters to the wrong zip code!"

"The wrong *zip code*?" Charlie Brown repeated.

Marcie nodded. "The zip code for the North Pole is 88888. These envelopes say 99999. You sent these letters to an address that doesn't exist!"

A smile spread across Charlie Brown's face. "If I hurry, the letters might make it to the North Pole before Christmas. Thanks, Marcie!" He took back the envelopes and rushed to the post office.

A few days passed. Charlie Brown checked his mailbox every day, but the letters never came back to him. They must have made it to the North Pole this time!

Charlie Brown had a feeling that it might be a great Christmas after all.

A Story for

Lucy's Long List

It was a very important day for Lucy Van Pelt. She had set aside the entire afternoon to write her letter to Santa to let him know what she'd like for Christmas. *What should I ask for this year?* Lucy wondered. She thought a bit, and then she got out a long sheet of paper. She started to write her list.

Dear Santa,
Thank you so much for the presents last Christmas. I hope you enjoyed giving them to me as much as I enjoyed receiving them. I am looking forward to my presents this Christmas. This year, I'd like a bicycle and a puppy and dolls. Oh, and also a camera and some candy and . . .

Lucy was so absorbed in her writing that she didn't notice Franklin walking by. Franklin was on his way to Charlie Brown's house to play a round of catch.

Franklin knocked on the front door. "Doing homework?" he asked Lucy.

"Oh, *no*," said Lucy, holding up her letter for Franklin to read. "This is *much* more important than homework. This is my letter to Santa! It's only the first draft, so please disregard any spelling errors."

Franklin started reading Lucy's letter. It was really long. He began to get worried he would be late to Charlie Brown's house. "You sure do have a lot of stuff on there, Lucy," he said.

"I think Santa appreciates a thorough letter," Lucy said. "And I don't want to leave anything out. After all, it's been a whole *year* since Santa brought me anything."

"It's nice to get presents from Santa on Christmas morning, but

Christmas is also about giving, not just getting," Franklin reminded Lucy. "What are you planning to give people this year?"

"Well, for starters, I'll be giving Santa this letter . . . ," Lucy began.

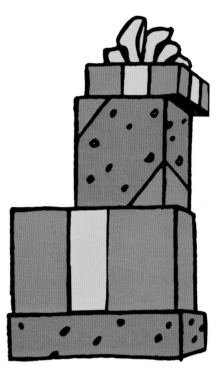

A Story for

December 3

Stocking Surprise

Charlie Brown and his sister, Sally, were putting up Christmas decorations. They had ribbons, ornaments, and most important of all . . . Christmas stockings! They could not wait to see what tiny trinkets Santa would put in their stockings this year.

"What do you hope Santa puts in your stocking this year?" Sally asked her brother. "I hope I get candy canes!"

"Uh . . . ," Charlie Brown started. Just then, he realized he didn't know *what* he wanted Santa to put in his stocking.

"Good grief, if I don't know what I want, how will Santa know?" Charlie Brown muttered to himself.

The next day at school, he asked his friends what types of stocking stuffers they were hoping Santa would bring them.

"Well, I'd really like some new markers so I can redecorate my booth," Lucy replied.

"And I'd love some ribbons for my hair! And maybe some new paint, too!" Violet added.

Charlie Brown headed back home after school, hanging his head down low. How could he not think of any good stocking stuffers? And he had to write his letter to Santa soon!

Then he spotted Snoopy out in the yard, decorating his doghouse.

"Snoopy," he said, putting his arm around him, "Christmas may look a lot different for me this year."

Snoopy gave Charlie Brown a confused look.

"I can't think of anything I want for Christmas, which means no one else will, which means I won't have anything in my stocking!" Charlie Brown exclaimed.

Snoopy licked Charlie Brown's face and nudged him to help decorate his doghouse.

"All right, all right," Charlie Brown said. Soon enough, he forgot about his stocking.

A few days later, Sally popped by her brother's room.

"You've got a present in your stocking already!" she exclaimed. "Santa must have filled your stocking early!"

Charlie Brown hurried over to his stocking. He peeked in to find . . . Snoopy!

"Oh, good grief," Charlie Brown said.

A Story for

December 4

Lucy's Big Day

Lucy was feeling very festive and in the holiday spirit. She was going to help Schroeder pick out his Christmas tree at a local farm!

"Oh, hi, Schroeder," Lucy cooed when he answered his front door. "Are you ready to go?"

"Why, most certainly," Schroeder replied. "Picking out a Christmas tree is one of my favorite things about the holidays. Well, that and playing Christmas songs on the piano, of course!"

The two friends walked to the farm. Soon they arrived. The farm looked like a winter wonderland. Trees were twinkling with lights and shiny ornaments. People were singing carols around a campfire and drinking hot cocoa with marshmallows.

Lucy, who usually did not show much emotion, could not help but beam at everything around her.

Schroeder, however, was distracted by a piano player nearby playing Christmas songs.

"Oh, good grief!" Lucy yelled. "Come on, let's go pick out a tree!"

They walked through a pathway lined with beautiful trees of all different shapes and sizes. Lucy was so excited to be spending time with Schroeder alone! *Maybe he will finally tell me how much he likes me,* she thought.

"Would you like a cookie?" Schroeder asked. Lucy smiled. This day was getting even better!

Just then, they heard a loud crash. It was Charlie Brown! He had flown his kite right into a very tall tree.

"Oh, hello, Charlie Brown," Schroeder said. "Want to help us pick out a tree?"

"Uh, sure, Schroeder," Charlie Brown muttered. He untangled himself from his kite.

"You blockhead!" Lucy shouted. Her perfect day with Schroeder was ruined!

A Story for

December 5

The Sibling Squabble

Lucy and Linus were walking to school. *And* they were fighting.

"You blockhead!" Lucy shouted.

"*Who's* a blockhead?" Linus shouted back.

"You're the blockhead!" Lucy shouted. "You and that blanket of yours."

"Oh yeah? Well, at least I'm not crabby all the time!" Linus said.

"Who's crabby?" Lucy yelled back.

The arguing went on for the entire walk to school. Charlie Brown was just about to walk into school when he heard the two of them arguing. *Oh no. Not again,* he thought.

"I can't believe it," Charlie Brown said. "Must you fight at Christmastime? What do you suppose Santa Claus is thinking about when he sees the two of you arguing all the time? Have you forgotten about his naughty and nice lists?"

Lucy turned pale, and Linus let out a gasp. Actually, they *had* forgotten about the naughty and nice lists!

Suddenly Lucy had an idea. She pulled Linus close and whispered into his ear. "Don't worry," she hissed. "*Trust* me, we can fool Santa. Just follow my lead."

Linus nodded. "Okay," he whispered.

Lucy looked at Linus and winked. Linus smiled at his big sister. Then Lucy suddenly grabbed Linus and gave him a huge hug!

"Oh, dear brother!" Lucy sang out.

"Oh, dear sister!" Linus cooed.

Now Lucy and Linus looked like the most loving brother and sister in the world! They walked into school holding hands.

Charlie Brown sighed. He knew it was fake, but what could he do? He shrugged. *Oh well,* he thought. *At least this is better than listening to them argue!*

A Story for

December 6

The Great Christmas Cookie Debate

Charlie Brown was so excited. His friend Franklin was coming over this afternoon to decorate Christmas cookies!

Before Franklin arrived, Charlie Brown started baking the cookies. Snoopy helped out too. They gathered flour, butter, sugar, and eggs. The ingredients went into a big bowl.

Snoopy hummed a Christmas carol while he mixed everything together to make a dough. Then Charlie Brown took the dough and rolled it out. They took turns using cookie cutters to make cookies shaped like Christmas trees, snowflakes, snowmen, and reindeer.

Snoopy tried to take a bite of a cookie. "No eating yet, Snoopy! We have to bake the cookies first," Charlie Brown said.

Franklin arrived while the cookies were baking in the oven. "Wow, those smell delicious!" he said.

After a while, the oven timer went off. But when Charlie Brown pulled the cookie sheet out, he discovered that all the cookies had crumbled apart into pieces!

"Oh no," Charlie Brown groaned. "What are we going to do now? Feed these crumbs to the dog?"

That sounds good to me! Snoopy thought.

"It's okay," Franklin said. "We can still eat them!"

"But *how*?" Charlie Brown said. "The cookies are totally ruined!"

Franklin pulled vanilla ice cream out of the freezer and scooped it into two bowls. Then he took a spoonful of the cookie crumbs and sprinkled it on top of the ice cream. He topped everything off with the decorations that were supposed to go onto the cookies: red and green sprinkles, crushed peppermint candies, and gumdrops.

Charlie Brown took a bite. "Wow, this is yummy, Franklin!" he said.

Then Franklin had another idea. They could invite their friends over to enjoy the cookie crumble ice cream too!

Soon some of their friends were gathered at Charlie Brown's house, decorating their own festive ice cream bowls.

"This is genius!" Lucy said. "How did you get the idea of crumbling the cookies?"

Franklin and Charlie Brown just looked at each other and laughed.

December 7

The Perfect Gift

Every year, Marcie and Peppermint Patty exchanged Christmas gifts. Every year, Marcie picked out a present for Peppermint Patty in the first week of December. Her presents were always thoughtful and perfect for Peppermint Patty. On the other hand, every year, Peppermint Patty raced around on Christmas Eve searching for something for Marcie. Two years ago she got Marcie a pair of socks. Last year she got Marcie a key chain that said HAPPY THANKSGIVING.

Well, this year, Peppermint Patty was determined *not* to wait until the last minute. So in the first week of December, she went to a place where she knew she'd find lots of things Marcie would like—the bookstore! Marcie loved books. All Peppermint Patty had to do was find a book on a subject that might interest Marcie.

But Peppermint Patty couldn't remember what her friend liked to read about. Did she like stories or poetry? History or science? All of the above? Peppermint Patty knew Marcie had interests, and she knew Marcie talked to her about them, but Peppermint Patty had a habit of not listening. "Rats," she said. "I'll just have to take a guess at what book Marcie might like."

So Peppermint Patty started by asking herself a question to which she would know the answer: "What kind of book would I want?" She wandered over to the sports section. There she saw the most interesting books she'd ever seen. Books filled with basketball stats!

Books about the world's greatest ice hockey players! Books on sports Peppermint Patty had never even heard of! She picked out a book that she wanted to read herself. "If it's perfect for me, it'll be perfect for Marcie," she said.

She had the present wrapped at the store and raced over to Marcie's house. "Merry Christmas!" she said when Marcie opened the door. She held out the present.

"Hello, sir," said Marcie. "I have a present for you too."

Marcie handed Peppermint Patty a package, and both girls ripped off the wrapping paper. Soon they were holding the same book in their hands—a how-to guide filled with insider tips on how to make a good baseball player even better.

"Oh, thank you, sir," said Marcie. "This is the best present you've ever gotten me. I'll start reading my copy right away. Maybe it'll teach me once and for all how to score a goal."

"That's a home run," Peppermint Patty corrected her.

"I know," said Marcie. "Scoring a goal would be a *real* home run!"

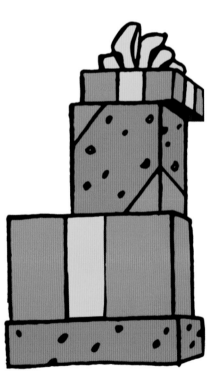

December 8

Woodstock's Decorating Dilemma

Woodstock loved the Christmas season. He loved flying around and seeing all the bright lights, feeling the crisp breeze through the air, and most of all . . . getting into the Christmas spirit. This year he planned to really go over the top with his nest decorations. He wanted to have the best nest in the neighborhood!

First, Woodstock flew around to check out the competition. Some birds had ornaments hanging off their nests, some birds had lots of twinkly lights, and some birds had ribbons tied to branches. But not one of them had a Christmas tree.

Woodstock chirped loudly. *That's it!* He would decorate his nest with a Christmas tree and a bright yellow star on top. It would be the perfect addition to his Christmas nest.

Woodstock circled around the forest in search of the perfect little tree. He spotted Franklin and Linus skating in the ice rink, and just to the right was a small tree peeking over the edge. It was the right size for his nest! He pulled out his tools and cut down the tree. Then he got his snow cart and dragged the tree over to his nest. Then he took a little snack break and had some cookies and hot chocolate before carrying his tree up to his nest. Before long, he was feeling quite tired, but he knew he had to finish decorating his nest. After all, he wanted to have the most decorated nest in the neighborhood!

After he added all the ornaments and lights, Woodstock was

completely wiped out. *How will I get the star on top?* he wondered.

Just then, his best friend Snoopy walked by. He clapped at Woodstock's tree. Then he noticed Woodstock lying in his nest, looking exhausted. Woodstock chirped at Snoopy in desperation. Snoopy knew just what to do. He grabbed his ladder and helped Woodstock with the final touch: he added the star to the top.

Woodstock grinned. Now he really felt in the Christmas spirit!

Thanks, Snoopy! Woodstock chirped. *Now my nest looks perfect, all thanks to the help from my best friend!*

What are best friends for? Snoopy responded with a grin. *I really hope you win the contest!* Then he heard a loud noise. His stomach was rumbling.

Since you're my best friend . . . and I helped you decorate your nest . . . , Snoopy began, *do you . . . happen to have any dog bones?*

That would make this day even more perfect, he thought. *And maybe some birdseed for my best friend Woodstock, too!*

A Story for
December 9

A Book for Charlie Brown

Charlie Brown loved Christmas cards, even though he didn't get many. Every day in December he eagerly checked the mailbox to see if any cards had come for him that day. Yesterday his favorite card came! It was his grandmother's card, which arrived every year a few weeks before the big day. She always included a thoughtful note and some money so, as she wrote, "you can buy something nice for yourself."

As Charlie Brown shoveled snow from his front walk that morning, he thought about what he should do with the money Grandma had sent him.

I could always save it for a rainy day, he thought. *Or the next snowy one. Speaking of snow, maybe I should buy a new shovel. If we have this much snow before Christmas, think of how much we'll get in January. It might be a good investment.*

"Hi, big brother!" shouted Sally, interrupting Charlie Brown from his thoughts. He was startled and fell back into a pile of snow.

"Hi, Sally," he said. "Can you help me up?"

Sally gave Charlie Brown her hand.

"What can I do for you, Sally?" Charlie Brown asked.

"Well, I was just wondering what you are going to buy with the money you got from Grandma for Christmas," she said.

"Oh, I don't know," said Charlie Brown. "I was thinking I could buy a new shovel. Or maybe a book."

Sally looked up at Charlie Brown sweetly. "You don't *really* want those things, do you, big brother? Wouldn't you rather combine our money so we could get something bigger?"

"Like a bigger shovel?" asked Charlie Brown.

"Or maybe something more fun," suggested Sally. "Something we could both enjoy!"

"What do you have in mind?" Charlie Brown asked her.

Sally took out some blueprints of a tree house. "I had these drawn up," she told Charlie Brown. "We could start working on it this spring."

Charlie Brown took a close look at the blueprints. At the top of the tree house, a sign said SALLY'S PLACE. STAY OUT!

Charlie Brown shook his head and handed the blueprints back to her. "I think I'd rather get a new book," he told her.

A Story for

A Sled for Linus

It was the first snowy day of winter, and all Linus wanted to do was to go sledding, so he grabbed the closest thing he had to a sled: a cardboard box. He just had to push it up the big, snow-covered hill, and then it would be smooth sledding all the way down to the bottom. He couldn't wait!

Then he realized something. *Pushing a cardboard box up a snow-covered hill is harder than I thought it would be,* thought Linus.

He even tried turning around and pushing the box up the hill while walking backward for a while. That was even harder!

When he finally made it to the top, he climbed into the box and took a seat. He was ready to go. He just wanted to take one quick look at the view.

He didn't know that Snoopy had noticed him and his box and was almost at the top of the hill too.

This view is spectacular! Linus thought as he looked out on the valley below. *I wish Snoopy were here to share it with me.*

Just then, the box began to wobble.

It tipped over, and Linus fell out . . . and he kept falling, and rolling, and somersaulting, all the way down to the bottom of the hill. It was a good thing that the ground was covered in snow!

He finally landed on his back and looked up at the hill, and he saw Snoopy sledding down the hill in the cardboard box. Snoopy was

gaining speed and heading straight toward Linus! They crashed . . .
and Linus, Snoopy, and the cardboard box all flew into the air.

When they landed, Linus was lying flat in the snow, the box was
upside down, and Snoopy was sitting on top of it and looking at Linus.
Christmas is coming, Snoopy thought. *You should ask for a sled.*
He was right.

December 11

Merry Christmas! Love, Snoopy

It was almost Christmas when Charlie Brown heard the doorbell ring. "I wonder who it could be," he said aloud, to no one in particular.

When he opened the door, he was delighted to see his pal Snoopy, smiling and holding out a gift with a big ribbon tied around it and a bow on top. He didn't know Snoopy was going to get him a present!

"For *me*?" Charlie Brown asked. Snoopy nodded. "Thank you very much!" He opened the card on top of the gift and read it aloud. "For the round-headed kid," Snoopy had written. "Merry Christmas."

The round-headed kid? Charlie Brown thought. *The round-headed kid! Is that the best he can do?*

"It would be nice to have a dog who remembered your name," Charlie Brown said aloud, hoping Snoopy would hear. *It would also be nice if he didn't make fun of things that make you who you are, like your big, round head,* he thought.

Then he looked up and realized that Snoopy had left.

Charlie Brown sighed. He wasn't even sure he wanted to open the gift anymore, but he was curious about what was inside, so he decided to do it anyway.

Inside there was a small picture frame that said, CHARLIE BROWN AND SNOOPY FOREVER!

Snoopy knows my name! Charlie Brown realized. *It's going to be a very merry Christmas after all.*

A Story for

December 12

Sally's Perfect Day

Sally was walking home when she saw Linus walking a few steps ahead of her. Just the person she wanted to see! Actually, he was the person she *always* wanted to see. She thought Linus was the most wonderful boy in the world. She hurried to catch up with him.

"Hello, Linus!" she said cheerfully. "In case you were wondering, my favorite color is blue."

"Hello, Sally," Linus said. "Why would I wonder what your favorite color is?"

"Because it's almost Christmas, silly," she replied. "And I'm sure you would like to give me a little gift, my Sweet Babboo."

Linus sighed. "Sally, I've told you a million times, I'm *not* your Sweet Babboo! I wish you wouldn't call me that. And I hope you aren't planning on getting me a gift, because even though we are good friends, I'm not planning on getting you something. I'm only buying gifts for my family this year."

Sally didn't say anything. She had already bought Linus a new pair of mittens. They were green, because she knew green was Linus's favorite color. She heard him tell Lucy once that green was his favorite color, and when someone is your Sweet Babboo, you remember things like that!

Linus didn't want Sally to feel bad. "I'll tell you what," he said. "It's supposed to snow tonight. If it does, would you like to go sledding tomorrow? I don't have my own sled, but I'll ask Lucy if I can borrow hers."

Sally beamed. "I would love that, my Sweet—I mean, Linus!"

The minute she woke up the next morning, she rushed to the window. It had snowed during the night! She called Linus, and they agreed to meet on top of the big hill near their school. She met Linus, and they went sledding together. They had a great time.

This is the best present ever, Sally thought. *Thank you, my Sweet Babboo!*

December 13

A School Surprise

Charlie Brown and Sally were at home writing Christmas cards.

Dear Linus, Sally wrote. *Merry Christmas to my Sweet Babboo! I will treasure you every year!*

Dear Lucy, Charlie Brown wrote. *This will be the Christmas I finally kick that football.*

Charlie Brown stopped and looked around. "Good grief," he said, wiping his brow. "We still have an awful lot of cards to write."

"Who else do we have to send cards to?" Sally asked.

"Well, we have to write one to our grandparents, to our friends, to Snoopy . . . ," Charlie Brown said.

"To your DOG?" Sally asked. "I'm not writing one to him!"

". . . and we have to send one to our teachers," Charlie Brown continued.

"OUR TEACHERS?!" Sally exclaimed. "Where do we send *their* Christmas cards?"

"Well . . . that's a good question," Charlie Brown said.

The next day at school, Sally and Charlie decided to find the answer. They asked their friends at lunch.

"Teachers live in school," Violet said. "That's why they know what day it is every day."

"No, no!" Lucy interrupted. "Teachers live in campers right outside of school. We just can't see them in the daytime. That's how they know whether we're coming to class or not. They spot us walking to school!"

"Teachers don't live anywhere," Linus said. "Just like the Great Pumpkin. They only appear when they're needed."

"I don't think any of that is right . . . ," Charlie said to Sally on their way home from school. "How will we send them Christmas cards if we don't know where they live?"

"Hey, Charlie Brown!" Pigpen called from behind them. "I know where teachers live!"

"Where, Pigpen? Tell us!" Sally said desperately.

"They live at home, of course," Pigpen said.

"At home? Teachers have *homes*?" Sally asked.

"Teachers have homes just like all of us," Pigpen said. "They celebrate Christmas with their families."

Charlie Brown and Sally looked at each other, shocked. Then they walked the rest of the way home and wrote Christmas letters to their teachers.

"Dear Teacher," Sally wrote. "I didn't know you had a home until today. Merry Christmas anyway!"

A Story for

December 14

Lucy's Santa Surprise

Lucy had a busy day planned. First she had to go to the library to return some cookbooks. Then she had to go to the post office to mail some Christmas cards. But most importantly, she had to go shopping. After all, Lucy was determined to pick out the perfect gift for Schroeder!

As Lucy daydreamed about Schroeder opening his perfect gift, she didn't notice that Santa Claus was nearby! But it wasn't the real Santa. It was Snoopy. He was being a Santa's helper for the day.

"Santa!" Lucy shouted. "You're just the person I need to see. Did you get my list? I hope so. I have LOTS of presents that I want this year. And I've been good this year. Well, pretty good. I mean, I'm sometimes nice to my brother, Linus. When he's not dragging around that stupid blanket, that is!"

Snoopy nodded and made some notes in his notebook.

"So you got my list, right, Santa?" Lucy asked again. "Because I really need a lot of the things I asked for! Like new paint for my booth! And some new saddle shoes. Oh, and a radio!"

But Snoopy just nodded again.

Lucy looked at Santa suspiciously. "Wait a minute," she said. "How come you haven't spoken yet?"

Snoopy just shrugged and gave Lucy a big grin.

"I don't get it!" Lucy exclaimed. "What is it? Cat got your tongue?"

Snoopy shook his head no. *Cats! Not a huge fan,* he thought.

Suddenly Lucy realized something. "Hey!" she shouted. "You look a lot like that blockhead Charlie Brown's dog, Snoopy!"

Snoopy blushed. Just then, a group of kids spotted him. "Santa!" they called.

Snoopy knew he had to move fast. He gave Lucy a kiss on the nose and ran away.

"Ew!" Lucy yelled. "I've been kissed by a dog dressed like Santa!"

December 15

A Sweater for Snoopy

Peppermint Patty liked a lot of things. She liked ice-skating and spending time with her friend Marcie. She also liked Chuck, whom almost everyone else called Charlie Brown.

She liked knitting, too, so she decided to make a Christmas gift for Chuck's dog, whom she called "that funny-looking kid with the big nose" and whom everyone else called Snoopy.

In the weeks leading up to Christmas, when Peppermint Patty wasn't ice-skating or spending time with Marcie, or getting yet another D-minus on a test, she was knitting.

She wanted to make the perfect Christmas sweater for Chuck's dog. She even learned how to knit a pattern with snowflakes and trees on it!

When it was finally ready, she folded it up, put it in a box, and sent it to Chuck. Then she called to make sure it had arrived safely.

"Hey, Chuck," Peppermint Patty said when Charlie Brown answered the phone. "Did your dog get the Christmas sweater I knitted for him?"

Charlie Brown had just helped Snoopy put on the sweater when he heard the phone ring. "Yes, thank you very much," he told Peppermint Patty.

"Did he like it?" she asked.

"Yes, he liked it . . . ," Charlie Brown told her.

"Was he wildly enthusiastic about it?" Peppermint Patty asked.

"Was he *what*?" Charlie Brown asked, thinking he must have been imagining the words he heard.

"Was he *wildly enthusiastic*?" Peppermint Patty said again.

Charlie Brown looked at Snoopy, or what he could see of him. The dog was covered from head to tail in a cocoon-shaped Christmas sweater that would have been perfect for a regular dog . . . but Snoopy was not a regular dog.

Snoopy's head hung low, and he was standing on all fours instead of on his hind legs like he usually did. He was not enthusiastic at all, but Charlie Brown did not want Peppermint Patty to know that, since she had worked so hard to make the sweater for Snoopy.

"Yes, he was wildly enthusiastic," Charlie Brown told Peppermint Patty, even though it wasn't true.

"That's great, Chuck," said Peppermint Patty. "Happiness is a warm puppy, so he must be feeling very warm now!"

And he was. In fact, Snoopy was so warm that when Peppermint Patty hung up the phone, Charlie Brown helped Snoopy take off the sweater . . . and Snoopy did his happy dance!

A Story for

December 16

A December Birthday

This Christmas, Lucy was more excited than ever. She had found the most perfect gift for Schroeder. It was a book of Mozart's compositions. She knew how much Schroeder loved music, and Mozart was a great composer. And she was going to give Schroeder his present today!

Lucy excitedly rang Schroeder's doorbell. "Oh, hi, Lucy," Schroeder said when he answered the door. "I have a surprise for you!"

"I have a surprise for you too!" She reached into her bag and pulled out the gift for Schroeder.

"Oh, that's so nice of you, Lucy!" he exclaimed. "Thank you. But first, let me show you my great surprise."

Schroeder brought Lucy into the living room, which was decorated for . . . a birthday party.

"Huh?" Lucy asked.

"Today is a *very* special day," Schroeder began. "It is the birthday of the world's greatest composer . . . Beethoven!"

Lucy gulped. *"Beethoven?"* she asked. "I thought Mozart was the world's greatest musical composer!"

"Well, he was very talented too," Schroeder said. "But no one compares to Beethoven!"

He grinned. "Now, should I open my gift?"

Lucy quickly grabbed the present from Schroeder. She would

have to go back to the bookstore and exchange it for a book about Beethoven!

"Oops, this one is actually meant for Linus," she stammered. "I'll have to come back with your present another day."

"That's okay, Lucy," Schroeder said. "Would you like some special Beethoven birthday cake?"

"Sure!" Lucy exclaimed. "Beethoven birthday cake is my favorite!"

A Story for

Dear Mr. Claus . . .

Snoopy was sitting on top of his doghouse. His typewriter was set up and ready to go, with a fresh piece of paper in it. Usually he used his typewriter to write chapters of the Great American Novel, but today he had a different kind of writing in mind: He was going to write the Great American Letter to Santa Claus! His friend Woodstock was there too, ready to help Snoopy make it the most perfect letter Santa had ever received.

Dear Santa Claus, Snoopy began to type. It sounded like a pretty good start to him, and he was about to go on to the next sentence when he heard chirping from Woodstock.

Woodstock wanted Snoopy to go in a more formal direction.

Snoopy decided to give it a try, and so he put a new piece of paper in the typewriter and used the greeting *Dear Mr. Claus* instead of *Dear Santa Claus.*

Woodstock started chirping again. *Dear Mr. Claus* wasn't quite what Woodstock had in mind. After all, what if Santa spoke French?

So Snoopy took out another new piece of paper and fed it through the typewriter. This time, he typed out *Dear Monsieur Claus* at the top of the letter, instead of *Dear Mr. Claus.*

Woodstock began to chirp again, and Snoopy sighed. Then Snoopy took the piece of paper out of the typewriter. This time, instead of throwing it out, he rolled it up into a tube.

Dear Monsieur Claus,

He put the tube of paper around Woodstock, who chirped in surprise.

Then Snoopy fed a new piece of paper into the typewriter and wrote, *Dear Santa Claus*. It was the perfect start to the Great American Letter to Santa Claus, after all.

Now, what else should I write? Snoopy asked Woodstock.

Woodstock began to chirp with all kinds of ideas. . . .

A Story for

December 18

The Candy Cane Mystery

Sally and her friend Eudora had a fun day planned. They were going to decorate Sally's Christmas tree!

"Hi, Eudora," Sally said when her friend arrived.

"Hello, Sally," Eudora replied. "Thanks so much for inviting me over. I brought you a special decoration for your tree!"

"Thanks!" she exclaimed. "Ooh, I love it!" Eudora had given Sally a Christmas ornament. It was shaped like a gingerbread cookie.

Eudora and Sally got right to work decorating the tree. They strung garlands of popcorn and cranberries, and hung ornaments and candy canes and tinsel.

"All this hard work is making me hungry," Sally said. "Want to go have a snack?" she asked Eudora.

"Thank you, Sally," Eudora said. "I could use a snack. I have hockey practice soon!"

Sally and Eudora headed to the kitchen. They had crackers with peanut butter and apples. They were so busy enjoying their snack that they didn't notice Snoopy and Woodstock sneaking into the living room.

A few minutes later, the girls were ready to finish decorating the tree. But something about the tree looked different.

"Hey!" Sally shouted. "Where did all the candy canes go?"

Eudora shook her head. "This is very strange," she said. "They were just here a few minutes ago! I could have sworn it."

The two friends looked under the tree, on the floor, and even under the couch cushions. But the candy canes weren't anywhere!

Just then, they heard music coming from outside. "Maybe Charlie Brown is outside," Sally said. "He can help us look for the candy canes!"

But when they went outside, Charlie Brown wasn't there. Snoopy was, though. And so were Woodstock and some of his bird friends. And so were the candy canes!

"Snoopy!" Sally shouted. "What are you doing with my candy canes?"

Snoopy grinned and did a tap dance. *What am I doing?* he thought. *Practicing for my Christmas musical, of course!*

December 19

Dear Samantha Claus . . .

Sally wanted to write a letter to someone special. She looked through the living room drawers, looking for some extra-fancy stationery. After some thought, she decided on a design with a blue snowflake border.

Then she wandered around the house, looking for a good pen. Charlie Brown's favorite pen was sitting on the dining room table. Sally took the pen, spread out the stationery, and sat down at the table. Now she was ready to start writing.

A few moments later, Charlie Brown walked into the dining room. "Have you seen my pen?" he asked.

"Nope," Sally replied.

Charlie Brown looked at his younger sister and the pen she was holding. He sighed. Then he sat down and peered at the letter. It said: *Dear Samantha Claus, how have you been?*

"*Samantha Claus?*" Charlie Brown repeated.

"She's the lady who brings us Christmas presents on a sleigh," Sally told him.

"Does Samantha Claus wear a red suit and have a white beard?" Charlie Brown asked.

"The white beard is just sort of a disguise," Sally replied.

Charlie Brown didn't know what to say except, "Very clever. . . ." He sat in silence for a few moments while his sister continued to write.

"How would you like it if I asked her to bring you a new bicycle?" Sally asked.

Charlie Brown shrugged and then nodded.

Please bring my brother a new bicycle, Sally wrote.

Then Charlie Brown asked, "Does Samantha Claus say, 'Ho, ho, ho' when she laughs? Or does she say, 'Who, who, who'?"

Sally stared at her brother. Then she shouted, "Children who make fun of Samantha Claus don't get presents!"

Turning back to the letter, Sally wrote, *Forget the bicycle!*

"Good grief," Charlie Brown sighed. It seemed like he wouldn't be getting a new bicycle after all. Unless, of course, Santa Claus brought him one. Maybe he would be kind enough to bring Charlie Brown a new pen, too!

A Story for

December 20

Pigpen's Special Gift

Pigpen woke up in a great mood. Today was the day of Violet's Christmas party! He couldn't wait to see all his friends, play holiday games, and eat yummy treats. He decided not to take a bath, but dressed in his most fanciest of outfits.

I bet no one will even recognize me, he thought.

When Pigpen arrived at the party, he was so excited to see all his friends. And he had brought a special gift for Violet. But he couldn't find her anywhere.

"Hello, Pigpen," Charlie Brown said politely. "That's a nice outfit you're wearing."

"Hi, Pigpen," Sally said. "We were just about to have a dance party. Want to join us?"

After the dance party, it was time for cookie decorating. Pigpen looked around for Violet, but it seemed she was busy either answering the door or talking to the other guests. *Oh well,* he thought. *I'll just have to give it to her later.* Pigpen started putting sprinkles and icing on a cookie shaped like a wreath.

"Move over, Pigpen!" Lucy shouted. "I can't decorate the cookies with all these clouds of dust!"

"I'm sorry, Lucy," Pigpen replied.

"Oh, never mind!" Lucy said. "I'm going to play a game!"

As she stomped away, Pigpen noticed that Violet was by a table of snacks, pouring a glass of punch and eating a gingerbread cookie.

Perfect! Pigpen thought. *Now I can give Violet her special gift!* He ran toward Violet.

"Merry Christmas, Violet," he said. "I brought you a very special gift. I hope you like it."

Violet grinned. "Gee, thanks, Pigpen," she said. She opened the box.

"Is this what I think it is?" Violet asked, coughing away clouds of dust.

"Yup!" Pigpen replied. "It's your very own bag of dust. Courtesy of yours truly!"

December 21

A Merry Bunny Christmas

It was a bright snowy day four days before Christmas. Charlie Brown was excited. Today he was going to make homemade Christmas cards for his friends with his best pal, Snoopy.

Charlie Brown put on his coat and snow boots and headed over to Snoopy's doghouse. Snoopy was still fast asleep.

"Wake up, Snoopy!" Charlie Brown called. "We have to get started on making our Christmas cards!"

Snoopy sat up and yawned. *Without having breakfast first?* he wondered.

"Oh, wait," Charlie Brown said. "I'm sure you would like your breakfast first." He gave Snoopy a big bowl of his favorite dog food.

That's more like it, Snoopy thought, chomping away happily.

After breakfast, it was time to start making Christmas cards! Charlie Brown set out a spread of construction paper, markers, stickers, sequins, and glue.

"Okay, Snoopy!" Charlie Brown said. "I'm going to start by making a card for Sally. What about you?"

Snoopy thought for a moment. *My best friend, Woodstock, of course!* he thought.

The two friends began to decorate their cards. Charlie Brown drew a giant Christmas tree on Sally's card. Snoopy drew a giant bird's nest filled with wrapped gifts for Woodstock. Then they made cards for

the rest of their friends. They were having such a fun time!

Soon they were ready to start delivering their cards. Their first stop was Peppermint Patty's house.

"Gee, thanks, Chuck," Peppermint Patty said as Charlie Brown handed her a card decorated with sports equipment drawn in red and green. "I love it!"

Snoopy then handed Peppermint Patty the card that he had made. Peppermint Patty looked at it curiously.

"Um, thanks, Snoopy," she said. Her card was yellow and was covered with flowers and bunnies. It looked more like an Easter card!

You're welcome, Snoopy thought, smiling. *Bunnies are my specialty!*

A Story for

December 22

The Perfect Gift Exchange!

Charlie Brown walked over to Snoopy's doghouse. He had a small gift-wrapped box in his hands. "Here, Snoopy. This is for you," he said.

Snoopy looked at the gift. There was a little card. *It's from Woodstock,* he said to himself. *How exciting! It's probably a fantastic gift,* he thought. *Woodstock does have great taste.*

Snoopy excitedly tore the wrapping paper off the package. When he opened it up, he was very surprised. It was . . . birdseed!

Why on earth would Woodstock give me birdseed? Snoopy wondered. *This is a terrible gift!* He was very disappointed. *Why would he give me something I can't use?* he said to himself. *At least I put a lot of thought into HIS present!*

Meanwhile, Woodstock was excitedly opening up his gift from Snoopy. He was sure Snoopy had bought him something wonderful.

Woodstock unwrapped his gift. It was . . . a dog bone!

Woodstock knew he had to be polite and say thank you. He would hide his disappointment and pretend he loved it. He brought the bone with him to Snoopy's doghouse. Snoopy was on top of his doghouse, holding his gift from Woodstock. When he saw Woodstock holding the yummy dog bone that Snoopy had given him, Snoopy suddenly had an idea. He hoped Woodstock would go for it.

Woodstock was just about to say thank you when Snoopy blurted out, *Do you want to trade?* Woodstock agreed immediately. They happily traded their gifts.

We give the best gifts, Snoopy thought.

December 23

A Story for Sally

It was two days before Christmas. Charlie Brown and Sally had had a great day.

First they had gone to visit their grandmother, who had made them a delicious pre-holiday lunch of ham, mashed potatoes, and their favorite biscuits. Sally and Charlie Brown had just gotten home and put on their coziest pajamas. Now it was time for stories by the fire!

Sally was excited. She had a very special Christmas book she wanted to read with Charlie Brown. But she couldn't find it anywhere! She looked under her bed, under the couch, and even under the Christmas tree. But there was no sign of it at all.

"Big brother!" Sally wailed. "I can't find my book. Story time is ruined!"

"I'll help you look, Sally," Charlie Brown said. But he couldn't find the book either.

Sally threw herself on the couch. "Everything is awful!" she cried. "I can't find my special book, and I haven't finished writing Christmas cards yet, and I still have to bake cookies for Linus!"

Charlie Brown thought for a moment. Then suddenly he had an idea.

"I know what we can do, Sally," he said. "I bought a new book with the money that Grandma sent me for Christmas. I was saving it for us to read tomorrow night, but how about we read it now?"

Sally smiled. "Are you sure, big brother? Even though you

were saving it to read on Christmas Eve?" She was starting to feel better already.

Charlie Brown nodded. "It will be a perfect ending to a perfect day."

Snoopy was excited to hear the story too. He jumped on top of the chair above Sally and Charlie Brown. He started snoring seconds later.

"It was a dark and snowy night," Charlie Brown began. "Santa and his reindeer were packing up the sleigh to begin their long journey of delivering presents to children all around the world. . . ."

December 24

Merry Christmas Eve!

"Tonight is the night!" Lucy shouted. "It's Christmas Eve! Tonight Santa Claus zooms around the world, dropping presents down the chimneys for all the little kids!"

Linus was excited too. But he was also concerned about Santa's long journey. "He sure has a lot of stops to make," he commented. "Do you think he'll have time to come to our house? I would understand if he doesn't."

"OF COURSE he will have time," Lucy snapped. "He is Santa Claus! He can do anything. Plus, he's got all those reindeer to help him out too."

"I hope his reindeer are up for making the trip," Linus said. "That sure is a lot of flying that they have to do."

"Why are you trying to ruin Christmas?" Lucy shouted. "His reindeer rest all year for the big trip. They will be fine!"

"They must get cold flying, especially when it snows. I hope they have a trusty old blanket to keep them warm like I do," Linus worried.

"Oh, good grief!" Lucy yelled. "You'll use any excuse to bring up that ratty old blanket. Why don't you leave it for the reindeer to take if you're so worried about them!"

"I'm a thoughtful person, but there's no way I can part with my blanket," Linus said solemnly.

"Can we stop talking about this blanket already? Come on and help me put out cookies and milk for Santa. And carrots for the reindeer too," Lucy said. "They also get hungry, you know!"

"That's a good idea," Linus said.

"Well, I'm so glad we can finally agree on something!" Lucy said. They put out a plate of cookies and a cold glass of milk for Santa. And a large dish of carrots for the reindeer.

"All right, all right, now let's go to bed," Lucy said. "Tomorrow's the big day!"

Linus did what he was told. "Merry Christmas Eve to all, and to all a good night," he said.

December 25

A Very Merry Christmas!

Finally the big day had arrived. It was Christmas Day! The Peanuts gang was so excited. After a busy morning spent opening gifts and having a yummy breakfast, they were going to meet at the park to go ice-skating, sing Christmas carols, and drink hot cocoa!

"Don't you just love the fluffy new scarf Santa brought me?" Sally asked Charlie Brown, throwing her scarf around her shoulders.

"It's very nice, Sally," Charlie Brown said. "I really like my new hat that he brought me, too."

Meanwhile, Lucy was anxious to get to the park. "Hurry up, Linus!" she shouted. "I want to try out my new ice skates!"

Schroeder was almost ready to leave for the park too. "I love the new songbook Santa got me," he said. "It will be perfect for keeping track of the new songs I write."

Soon everyone had arrived at the park.

"Merry Christmas, Chuck," Peppermint Patty told Charlie Brown. "Do you like my new hockey stick?"

"Can we get on with the Christmas carols already?" Lucy shouted. "I really want to go ice-skating!"

Sally and Marcie handed out hot cocoa to everyone, and they all gathered around the Christmas tree, singing their favorite carols. It was the best Christmas Day ever!

Merry Christmas!